Shrek the Halls

Copyright © 2008 by DreamWorks Animation L.L.C.

Printed in the United States of America.

All rights reserved. No part of this book may be used or reproduced in any manner whatsoever without written permission
except in the case of brief quotations embodied in critical articles and reviews.

For information address HarperCollins Children's Books, a division of HarperCollins Publishers,
1350 Avenue of the Americas, New York, NY 10019.

www.harpercollinschildrens.com

Library of Congress catalog card number: 2007933231

ISBN 978-0-06-143078-7

Book design by Rick Farley and Joe Merkel

❖

First Edition

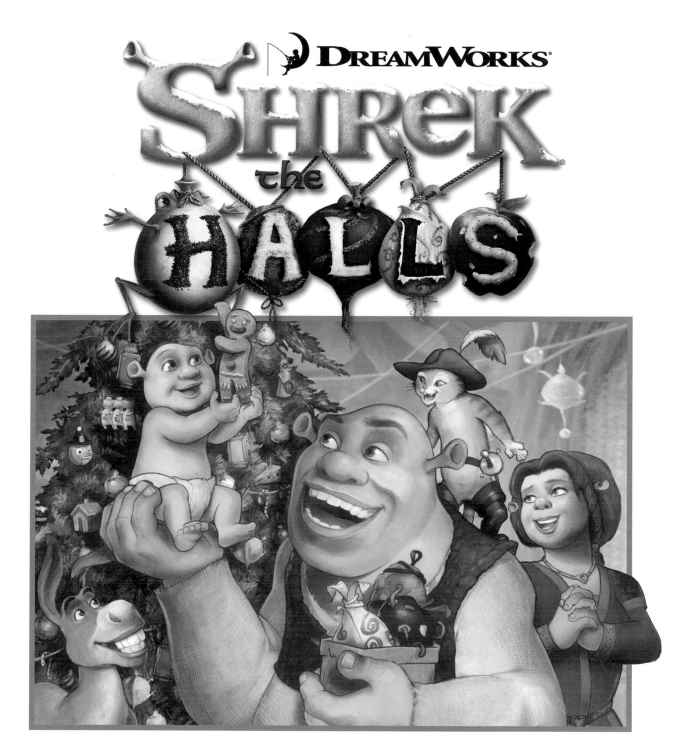

Adapted by Catherine Hapka

Illustrated by Mike Sullivan and Michael Koelsch

HarperCollins Publishers

One fine summer day, Shrek was soaking up the sun and watching his babies play in the mud. Everything was perfect...until Donkey showed up.

"Only one hundred and fifty-nine days left till Christmas," Donkey sang out. "So you'd better be good!"

Shrek glared at him. "*You'd* better be scarce," he said. "I don't care about Christmas."

One hundred and fifty-seven days later, Donkey was still pestering Shrek about Christmas.
He was horrified to learn that Shrek wasn't prepared.

"You mean you haven't trimmed your stockings, hung your chestnuts, or roasted the tree?"

"Get it through your thick head," Shrek said. "No one here gives a hoot about—"

Just then Fiona wandered by, holding the babies. "Your first snow!" she cooed happily.

"And just in time for Christmas!"

Shrek was surprised to see her so excited.

Shrek didn't know the first thing about Christmas! But if it was important
to Fiona, it was important to him, too.

That night, he sneaked off to the village bookstore. Luckily the store had just
the book he needed. It showed everything Shrek needed for a perfect Christmas.

He just hoped he could pull it off.

Shrek got up early the next morning to decorate the swamp. He didn't have most of the stuff shown in his book, so he had to get creative.

"It's beautiful!" Fiona said when she saw Shrek's decorations.

"It's horrible!" Donkey had just arrived on the scene. "Don't worry, Princess," he told Fiona. "Shrek's going to want my help."

"Actually," Fiona said, "Shrek really wants a nice *family* Christmas."

The family set out to gather more decorations. "This is going to be the best Christmas ever," Fiona said cheerfully. "And we're going to do it together! Come on!"

They set off into the woods, pulling the babies on a sled. It turned out Fiona could get creative, too! She showed Shrek how to belch on snakes to make them look like candy canes. The babies even helped by blowing up lizard balloons.

Soon they'd found plenty of decorations.

Finally the house looked *almost* like the pictures in Shrek's book.

"It's perfect," Shrek said with relief as he and his family relaxed in front of the fire. "And now, it's story time… '*Twas the night before Christmas, and all through the house…*'"

The door burst open. "Merry Christmas, Shrek!" Donkey cried. He rushed in, followed by all the fairy-tale friends.

"Happy holidays!" Pinocchio cried, doing a Christmas jig.

"Nice to see you, Fiona," one of the Three Little Pigs added. Greetings filled the house as more and more friends swarmed in.

"What a nice surprise!" Fiona exclaimed.

"Oh yeah," Shrek grumbled.

He couldn't believe it— his perfect family Christmas had just turned into a crazy, crowded party!

Shrek tried to sneak away to tell his babies their Christmas story, but Donkey overheard.

"Are you telling *The Night Before Christmas?*" he cried. "I tell it better than anybody! Gather 'round, everybody."

He recited a wild version about a big Christmas parade and a fifty-foot Santa made of waffles.

Then Gingy interrupted, looking upset. "Where
I come from, Christmas is a nightmare!" he cried. He told
a scary story about a giant, hungry Santa.

Finally Shrek had had enough. This was *not* how he'd planned his perfect family Christmas!

"Out!" he yelled. "I want everybody out of my house right now!"

Donkey was thrown out the window and landed with a splat. The rest of the fairy-tale friends hurried out behind him.

"Nice way to treat your guests on Christmas, Ebenezer Shrek!" Donkey huffed. "If you think I'm going to give you a present now, you're *sadly* mistaken!"

Finally Shrek was happy, but Fiona wasn't. She rushed out the door to apologize to their friends.

"But I wanted a perfect family Christmas," Shrek said.

"That *was* our family!" Fiona exclaimed as she stomped off with the babies.

Shrek thought about it and realized she was right. Besides, maybe *perfect* was overrated.

He caught up with Fiona and their friends and apologized.

"It would mean a lot to me if you'd all come back," he said. "What do you say?"

Soon the Christmas party was back in full swing. This time, Shrek
even got to tell *his* own version of *The Night Before Christmas*.
And it was perfect!

The Night Before Christmas
(SHREK STYLE)

 'Twas the **night** before
Christmas
and not a **swamp** rat did **creep**,
as mother and babe played **kazoo**
in their sleep.

NOW, the sight of **the house**
would make any **ogre** droop,
for 'twas **sickeningly** sweet as
unicorn poop.

Yet **who was** arriving
to help this **lost cause?**
The foul, the **vile**, and **handsome**
(heh heh) **Ogre Claus!**

He looked **all** around
and **scratched** at his beard,
and **said**, "This place is **worse**
than I thought, uh, **feared.**"

So he revved up his belly
and screwed up his face
and let loose a belch
that transformed the place!

With a gleam in his eye,
his work here was done.
And then to the babies
he gave one by one—

A festering bottle
of stinky swamp juice,
and for Mommy a kiss
and a good Christmas goose.

Then, digging a finger
inside of his nose
and giving a nod,
up the chimney he rose.

And I heard him exclaim
as he drove out of sight,
"Smelly Christmas to all,
and to all a gross night!"